For Ellie

SIMON & SCHUSTER BOOKS FOR YOUNG READERS

An imprint of Simon & Schuster Children's Publishing Division

1230 Avenue of the Americas, New York, New York 10020

Copyright © 2020 by Elizabeth Rose Stanton

SIMON & SCHUSTER BOOKS FOR YOUNG READERS is a trademark of Simon & Schuster, Inc.

For information about special discounts for bulk purchases, please contact Simon & Schuster

Special Sales at 1-866-506-1949 or business@simonandschuster.com.

The Simon & Schuster Speakers Bureau can bring authors to your live event. For more information or to book an event,

contact the Simon & Schuster Speakers Bureau at 1-866-248-3049 or visit our website at www.simonspeakers.com.

Book design by Alicia Mikles

The text for this book was set in Myster.

The illustrations for this book were rendered in pencil and watercolor.

Manufactured in China

1019 SCP

First Edition

2 4 6 8 10 9 7 5 3 1

Library of Congress Cataloging-in-Publication Data

Names: Stanton, Elizabeth Rose, author, illustrator.

Title: Cowie / Elizabeth Rose Stanton.

Description: First edition. New York : Simon & Schuster Books for Young Readers, 2020. "A Paula Wiseman Book."

Summary: A donkey wants to be a cow but needs his animal friends to help him learn how to moo first.

Identifiers: LCCN 2019006398 ISBN 9781534421745 (hardcover) ISBN 9781534421752 (eBook)

Subjects: CYAC: Cows—Fiction. Donkeys—Fiction. Individuality—Fiction. Animal sounds—Fiction.

Classification: LCC PZ7.S79326 Co 2020 DDC E —dc23

LC record available at https://lccn.loc/.gov/2019006398

Cowie

Elizabeth Rose Stanton

A PAULA WISEMAN BOOK · SIMON & SCHUSTER BOOKS FOR YOUNG READERS

New York London Toronto Sydney New Delhi

This is Cowie.

Everyone called him Cowie

because Cowie loved everything about cows.

He admired their soft ears
and their kind eyes.

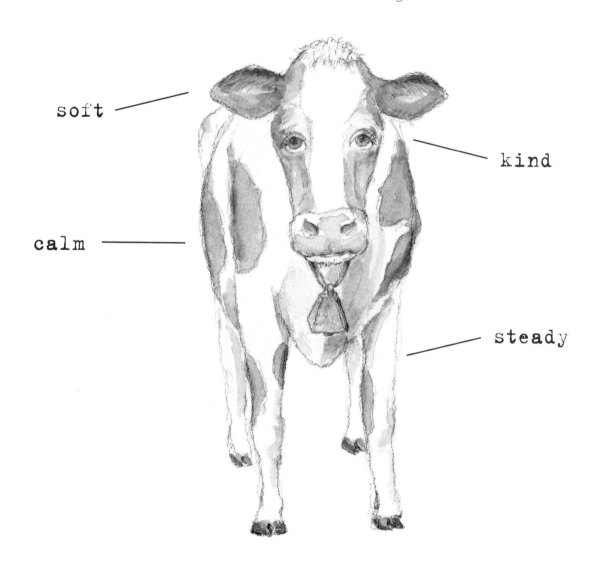

soft

kind

calm

steady

COW (contented)

He saw how content they were . . .

how calm and steady.

COWIE (in love)

And Cowie especially admired
the peace and quiet,
and green, green grass
on *their* side of the fence.

No one rode them,

or made them carry things,

or made them pull things around.

Me

One day, Cowie decided
the time had come.

If I stand with the cows, he thought, *I will be a cow.*

Cowie stood with the cows.

Not much happened.

Cowie thought some more:

If I act like a cow, I will surely be a cow.

So, while standing among the cows,

he chewed some cud.

He swished his tail at the flies, and he nibbled

at their green, green grass.

Still, nothing changed.

I know, thought Cowie . . . I will say MOO.

Then I will certainly be a cow!

Cowie drew in a big, big breath.

Out came:

OOOOOOM

Everyone stopped chewing
and swishing and mooing
and looked at Cowie.

I am making too much of a donkey *of myself,* he thought.

I will never be a cow.

"What's wrong, Cowie?"

asked his friends, Duckie and Mousie.

Cowie answered with a long

and unhappy,

OOOOOooM

Duckie and Mousie wanted to help their friend feel better.

"Look, Cowie!" squeaked Mousie.

"I will say K-A-E-U-Q-S."

KAEUQS

squeak

"Your turn, Duckie!"

In his best fowl voice,

Duckie shouted,

KCAUQ

quack

But it didn't make Cowie feel better–

because everyone knows

Q has to come before U for it to come out right.

NO	YES
uqick	quick
suqare	square
euqal	equal
uqeen	queen
uqiz	quiz

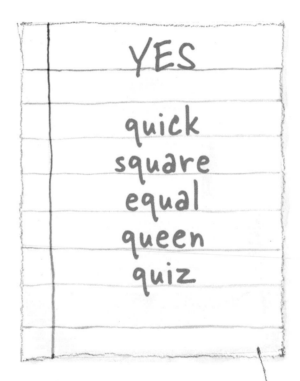

So Duckie and Mousie went back to
quacking and squeaking . . .
and wanting to help their friend.

OOM

Next, Duckie and Mousie decided
they'd better check Cowie
from hoof to head.

When they got to his head:

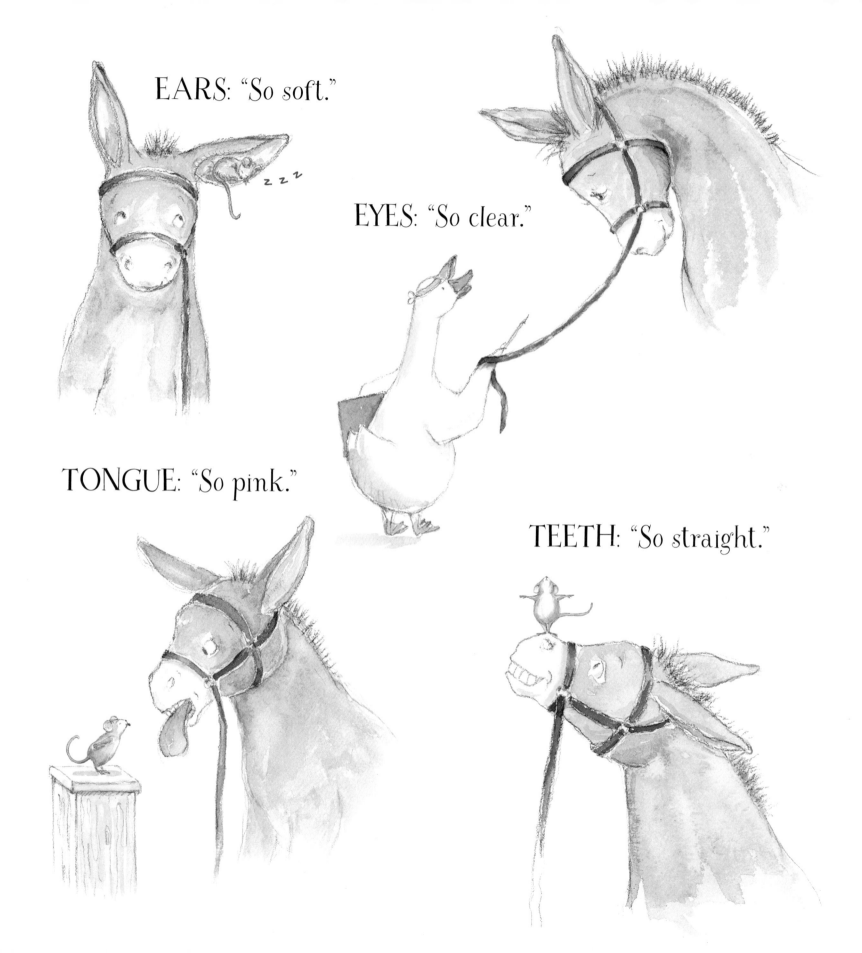

EARS: "So soft."

EYES: "So clear."

TONGUE: "So pink."

TEETH: "So straight."

BREATH:

"WHOA!"

So they brushed his teeth,
and gave him a mint.

"Give it a try now, Cowie!"

Cowie took in a big breath

and out came

a very fresh and minty

OOOM

The friends sat and thought for a while . . .

then Mousie had an idea!

"Try it this way, Cowie!"

said Mousie.

This time, Duckie and Mousie noticed something.

Do you see what I see?

WOO WOO

"Cowie! Try shouting, 'MOO!'
as LOUD as you can!"

And it became clear what needed to be done!

They took turns taking turns,

until everything turned around, just right, for Cowie.

After a brief and
happy celebration, he mooed
the rest of his days away—

a contented Cowie . . .

if there ever was one.

MOOOOO